"A sensitive and poignant tale to aid and support children who may be facing an untreatable illness. *The Night Crossing* can help soften the fear about the journey into the unknown."

Hephzibah Kaplan, Art Therapist, Director of London Art Therapy Centre

"*The Night Crossing* is so sensitively written, with beautiful illustrations. I found it honest and touching, a sympathetic aid that could be revisited whenever needed. In our experience, children take in as little or as much as they feel comfortable to deal with when they are ready. I also feel this book could help siblings of a child who is very ill and for parents or carers to help gauge other children's questions and emotions."

Family member, Anonymous

"As children are so naturally at ease with metaphor, I imagine *The Night Crossing* could answer some of the unspoken fears of a child and families at this time with honesty and kindness. It acknowledges the wisdom of the child who in his heart knows what is happening. I would also hope that this story could open up the possibility of conversations between parent and child. A touching and sensitive work, with beautiful illustrations."

Anna Ledgard, Arts Producer, End of Life doula trainer

"A sensitively written and delightfully illustrated book that provides support and comfort to both a seriously ill child or siblings. *The Night Crossing* provides a safe space for parents and professionals to explore the fears and emotions a child may experience but also provides the opportunity for a child to ask difficult questions."

Janey Treharne, Jigsaw, South East

"This book has done something very beautiful and reassuring with a very difficult topic."

Taylor Smart, Art Psychotherapist

T0002825

The Night Crossing

This beautifully illustrated and sensitive storybook is designed to be used therapeutically by professionals and caregivers supporting children with an untreatable illness. With engaging, gentle and colourful illustrations that can be used to prompt conversation, it tells the story of the final journey made by a Boy with a Bear, as the Boy says his goodbyes and comes to terms with his life-ending illness.

This book is also available to buy as part of the *Therapeutic Fairy Tales* set. *Therapeutic Fairy Tales* is a series of short modern tales dedicated to exploring challenging life situations that might be faced by children. Each short story is designed to be used by professionals and parents as they use stories therapeutically to support children's mental and emotional health.

Other books in the series include:

- *Storybook Manual: An Introduction To Working With Storybooks Therapeutically And Creatively*
- *The Storm: For Children Growing Through Parents' Separation*
- *The Island: For Children With A Parent Living With Depression*

Designed to be used with children aged 6 and above, each story has an accompanying online resource, offering therapeutic prompts and creative exercises to support the practitioner. These resources can also be adapted for wider use with siblings and other family members.

The Night Crossing – part of the *Therapeutic Fairy Tales* series – is born out of a creative collaboration between Pia Jones and Sarah Pimenta.

Pia Jones is an author, workshop facilitator and UKCP integrative arts psychotherapist, who trained at The Institute for Arts in Therapy & Education. Pia has worked with children and adults in a variety of school, health and community settings. Core to her practice is using arts and story as support during times of loss, transition and change, giving a TEDx talk on the subject. She was Story Director on artgym's award-winning film documentary, 'The Moving Theatre,' where puppetry brought to life real stories of people's migrations. Pia also designed the 'Sometimes I Feel' story cards, a Speechmark therapeutic resource to support children with their feelings. You can view her work at www.silverowlartstherapy.com

Sarah Pimenta is an experienced artist, workshop facilitator and lecturer in creativity. Her specialist art form is print-making, and her creative practice has brought texture, colour and emotion into a variety of environments, both in the UK and abroad. Sarah has over 20 years' experience of designing and delivering creative, high-quality art workshops in over 250 schools, diverse communities and public venues, including the British Library, V&A, NESTA, Oval House and many charities. Her work is often described as art with therapeutic intent, and she is skilled in working with adults and children who have access issues and complex needs. Sarah is known as Social Fabric, www.social-fabric.co.uk

Both Pia and Sarah hope these *Therapeutic Fairy Tales* open up conversations that enable children and families' own stories and feelings to be seen and heard.

Therapeutic Fairy Tales

Pia Jones and Sarah Pimenta

978-0-367-25108-6

This unique therapeutic book series includes a range of beautifully illustrated and sensitively written fairy tales to support children who are experiencing trauma, distress and challenging experiences, as well as a manual designed to support the therapeutic use of story.

Titles in the series include:

Storybook Manual: An Introduction To Working With Storybooks Therapeutically And Creatively
978-0-367-49117-8

The Night Crossing: A Lullaby For Children On Life's Last Journey
978-0-367-49120-8

The Island: For Children With A Parent Living With Depression
978-0-367-49198-7

The Storm: For Children Growing Through Parents' Separation
978-0-367-49196-3

The Night Crossing

A Lullaby For Children On Life's Last Journey

Pia Jones and Sarah Pimenta

Routledge
Taylor & Francis Group

LONDON AND NEW YORK

First published 2021
by Routledge
2 Park Square, Milton Park, Abingdon, Oxon OX14 4RN

and by Routledge
52 Vanderbilt Avenue, New York, NY 10017

Routledge is an imprint of the Taylor & Francis Group, an informa business

British Library Cataloguing-in-Publication Data
A catalogue record for this book is available from the British Library

Library of Congress Cataloging-in-Publication Data
Names: Jones, Pia, author. | Pimenta, Sarah, illustrator.
Title: The night crossing : a lullaby for children on life's last journey / Pia Jones and Sarah Pimenta.
Description: Abingdon, Oxon ; New York, NY : Routledge, 2020. | Series: Therapeutic fairy tales | Summary: Accompanied by a reassuring Bear, a young Boy takes a final journey as he comes to terms with his life-ending illness. Includes a note on how to use the book as a therapeutic resource.
Identifiers: LCCN 2020001471 (print) | LCCN 2020001472 (ebook) | ISBN 9780367491222 (hbk) | ISBN 9780367491208 (pbk) | ISBN 9781003044666 (ebk)
Subjects: CYAC: Terminally ill--Fiction. | Death--Fiction.
Classification: LCC PZ7.1.J726 Ni 2020 (print) | LCC PZ7.1.J726 (ebook) | DDC [E]--dc23
LC record available at https://lccn.loc.gov/2020001471
LC ebook record available at https://lccn.loc.gov/2020001472

ISBN: 978-0-367-49120-8 (pbk)
ISBN: 978-1-003-04466-6 (ebk)

Typeset in Calibri and Antitled
by Servis Filmsetting, Stockport, Cheshire

Visit the eResources: www.routledge.com/9780367491208

Acknowledgements

A special thank you to Stuart Lynch for all the time and creative support he generously gave to *The Night Crossing*. Thanks to Hephzibah Kaplan, for her enriching input and ideas.

Thanks to Speechmark for looking after our fairy tales so well and turning them into such beautiful books. A special mention also to our editor, Katrina Hulme-Cross, for her calm, steady guidance, and all her support for these stories. And to Leah Burton, Cathy Henderson and Alison Jones for taking our books into production with such care and attention.

Thanks to all the other people who have supported us along the journey: Alastair Bailey, Katrina Hillkirk, Annie Duarte, Molly Wolfe, Fiamma Ceccomori-Jones, Sarah Farr, Tamsin Cooke, Jacob Pimenta-Richardson, Antonella Mancini, Daniele Ceccomori and Alex Poole.

A word of caution

Before starting *The Night Crossing*, please take a moment to read

The Night Crossing has been especially written for children making their final goodbyes to families and loved ones due to untreatable illness. The book is designed to serve as a therapeutic resource to support children with their personal, emotional journeys alongside an adult reader.

Given the sensitive subject matter, *The Night Crossing* may provoke strong responses. For this reason, it's important the book is read in the right setting, with respect and due care for the child's well-being and energy levels, leaving ample time for feelings and reflections. This is not a story that can be rushed.

For the adult reader, professional or non-professional, it is advisable to read this story first alone, to ensure you have time to process your own emotions in order to prepare for supporting your child reader.

For extra resources on how to work with this story, and examples of creative exercises, please go to the online resources: www.routledge.com/9780367491208. For ideas on how to work with story and image in general, please refer to our *Storybook Manual: An Introduction To Working With Storybooks Therapeutically And Creatively*: www.routledge.com/9780367491178.

Once upon a time, there was a young Boy who lived with his family by a lake. The Boy loved being in nature playing outside with his friends.

One day, the Boy was climbing over a fallen tree when he was bitten by a snake. Before anyone could catch it, the snake disappeared, nowhere to be seen.

The poison went straight into the Boy's blood. It made him feel very tired and unable to do the things he enjoyed, like fishing and playing with friends.

The young Boy had to rest and meet lots of doctors and nurses. They tried all sorts of medicines to help, but the venom was too strong. His family did their best to make the Boy feel comfortable, but no one could stop him from becoming very ill.

One evening, when the Boy had been asleep most of the day, he heard a gentle tapping from his bedroom window. Slowly sitting up, the Boy blinked in disbelief. There was a strange light shining right through it.

Facing him, was a giant silver-white bear, with deep-brown eyes – the colour of warm melted chocolate.

The Boy rubbed his own eyes. The silver-white bear smiled and waved to the Boy to open the window. The Boy could just about push it open and shivered as a breeze blew in.

"Hello," said the Bear in a very ordinary sort of way.

"You're a bear," said the Boy, feeling exhausted, and not quite sure if he were awake or dreaming.

The Bear's bright silver fur looked like it was lit from within. Maybe one of the Boy's medicines was making him see funny things.

"Bear by name and bear by nature," answered the Bear kindly. "I'm here to take you on a trip, somewhere safe."

"I can't, I'm too ill," said the Boy sadly, because the fur on the Bear looked so very soft and so very silver. It was a long time since he'd been able to go anywhere.

"Don't worry, I'll carry you," said the Bear. "How about putting on your dressing gown to keep warm."

The Boy's heart thumped. With a nod, he slowly pulled on his dressing gown and slippers.

"Here, let me help you climb up," said the Bear, seeing the Boy stumble.

The Bear's fur was warm as well as soft, and the Boy tucked both hands inside to feel its heat.

"You're so toasty," whispered the Boy, holding on as tight as he could. "Don't drop me, or my Mum will never forgive you."

"I know," said the Bear with a smile, "You are precious."

The Bear climbed out of the window carefully. His heavy paws padded on the grass in front. Seeing how well the Bear looked after him, the Boy began to relax his grip.

"Where are we going?" asked the Boy, yawning widely.

"Not so far," said the Bear. "Rest now …"

The Boy laid down his head between the Bear's strong shoulders and before he knew it, he had been rocked to sleep.

After a while, the Boy woke up to the sound of water lapping. The moon had come out and shone on a rowing boat waiting by the shore. It was a part of the lake that the Boy didn't know.

As the Boy was carried into the boat, he noticed there was a tree, a weeping willow. Its leaves were falling one by one, floating down to the water. Some of the leaves fluttered into the boat. The Bear gently laid the Boy down inside, on a bed of warm blankets.

"Mmmm, I like this," said the Boy, pulling the soft material over him. "It's like my very own nest."

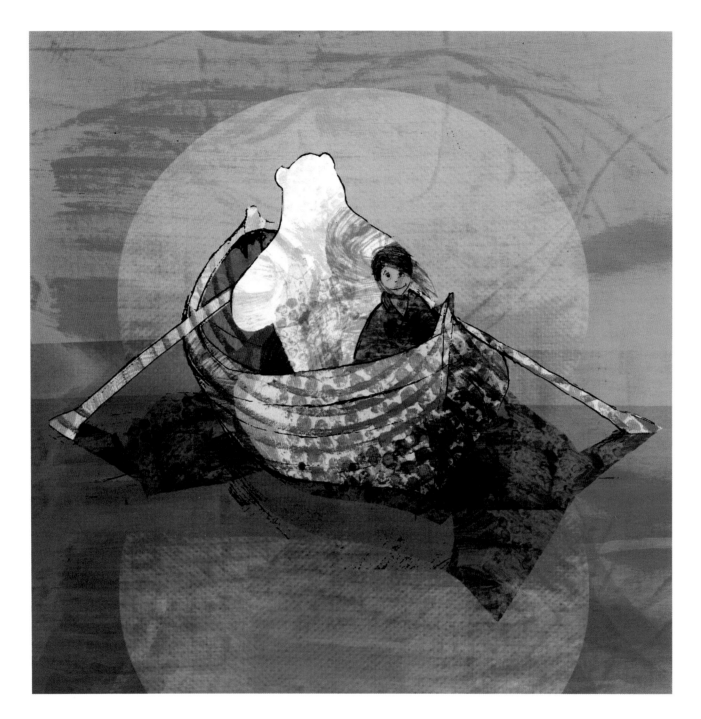

The Bear sat at the bow of the boat and picked up the oars. There was a gentle *whoosh* as the wooden blades moved through the water. The Boy could feel his eyes shutting again.

A deep sleep was calling the Boy, almost too strong to resist. As he started to slip into it, the figures of his family, friends and teachers, appeared. They stood on the shore waving at him, faces filled with love and longing. As he also waved, a sudden thought woke him up again.

"I'm not coming back, am I?" said the Boy, calling up to the Bear.

There was a long silence before the Bear answered.

"No," said the Bear sadly, his voice sounding as old as Time itself.

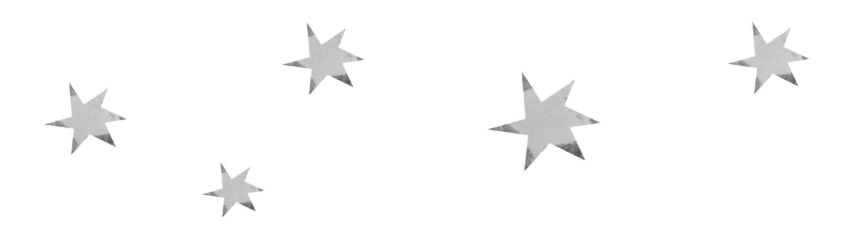

"Oh," sighed the Boy, pulling the blankets close, looking up at the stars twinkling above.

The Boy and the Bear travelled in silence for a while, listening to the oars travel through the water. The Boy closed his eyes and nestled into the soft blankets. His heart felt heavy as stone.

21

After a while, the Boy spoke again, "No one can come with me, can they?"

The Bear leant over and stroked his head, tears in his eyes. "No, they can't, not now. It's not their time."

Nodding, the Boy reached up to the Bear. They looked into each other's eyes. The Bear seemed to know the mysteries of the world, and the Bear thought the same of the Boy.

"What can I take with me, I wonder?" asked the Boy, when he finally let go of the Bear.

He looked up at the fading stars and closed his eyes. A deep sleep was pulling him now, the deepest of all. Snuggling under the blankets, the Boy felt a strange sensation. It was a feeling of hands outstretched beneath him, the hands of people gone before him, young and old, reaching to support and greet him.

"I know what I take with me," said the Boy to the Bear, with a sigh. "I take stories with me. I take the stories of my life that I have shared with my family and friends. I take the stories and memories of all who have been important to me."

"And you are held in the stories and memories of those you are leaving, and who, one day, will follow you," added the Bear softly. "You will not be forgotten."

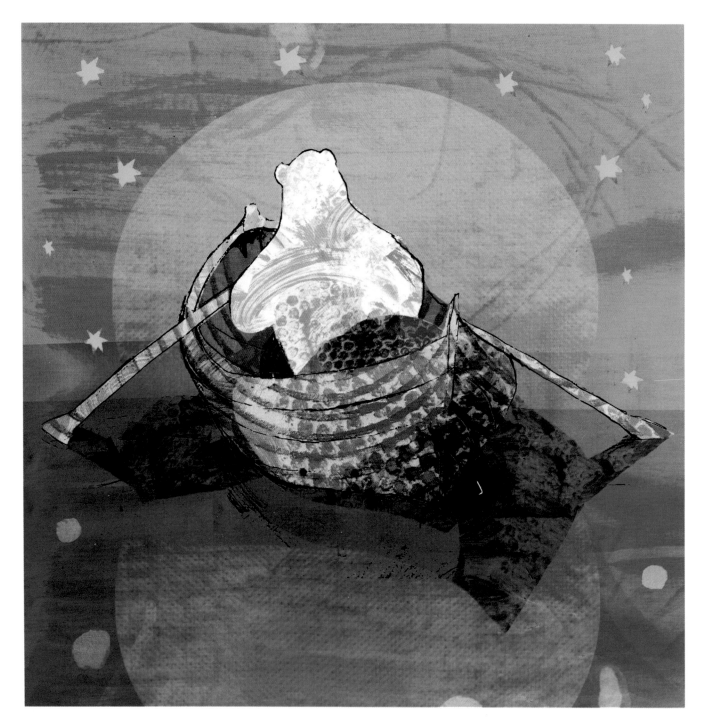

As the Boy turned over in his nest of blankets and took his last breath, the stars twinkled, and the light of the moon showed the Bear the way.